The Princess
in the Kitchen Garden

For Mother

❧ The Princess ❧
in the Kitchen Garden

Annemie & Margriet Heymans

Translated by

Johanna H. Prins and Johanna W. Prins

Farrar, Straus and Giroux

New York

WHEN THE SCHOOL BUS dropped him off at home, Matthew ran straight to his father's room.

"I passed!" he called. "Look here, it says so on my report card."

" 'Matthew is promoted to the next grade,' " Father read out loud, " 'but PENMANSHIP NEEDS IMPROVEMENT.' " He called Hannah in and said, "Hannah, choose a book from your bookcase and see to it that your brother copies two pages out of it every day."

"Two pages! That's an awful lot," Matthew protested. "I need to play, too!"

But Father did not give in. "Your schoolwork is more important and that's that," he said.

Matthew sat at his desk, with his nose in a book and a pen in his mouth. It was the first day of summer vacation. Twice he yelled, "ALL THE KIDS CAN PLAY EXCEPT ME!" But no one heard him.

Not Hannah, because she was downstairs scrubbing and cleaning.

Not Father, because he was, as always, busy in his room: writing and calculating, erasing and correcting, ripping the paper to shreds or cutting off the edges. If anyone asked him why, he would say, "Because it has to be done."

While Matthew was lying in bed that evening, Hannah looked in his notebook.

"Why is it empty?" she asked.

But Matthew didn't answer. He was asleep.

Hannah shrugged and went downstairs.

"Father?" asked Hannah.

"Hm?"

"I put Matthew to bed. He hasn't had a good-night kiss from you."

"Oh?"

"I've made you some hot chocolate, because we're out of coffee."

"Yes, yes."

"Today I did the dishes and hung the laundry…I ironed your shirts…The goat ate your hat…There's a wolf in the kitchen!…THE SHED'S ON FIRE!"

"Have you made coffee for me yet?" asked Father.

"I'm running away! I'm going to Mama's garden!"

"Did you say something, Hannah?"

"No, Father. Nothing."

It's so quiet in the house.
I can't hear Hannah.
I just hear the birds singing.
Maybe she's still asleep.
Or maybe she's sick.

Dear Matthew,
  Don't look for me. You
won't be able to find me.
Remember your homework!
First read the story carefully,
then copy it neatly. Don't
cross the ditch, because on the
other side there's a dangerous
swamp.

  Hannah

She's not in her bed.   "Koos, have you seen Hannah?"

"Really, her hand-
writing isn't so neat,
either."

Dear Matthew,
  In the Forbidden Room—Mama's
room—is a wicker basket. I need
it. Bring it to the ditch. Then
go back home right away.
         Hannah
P.S. The key is under the doormat.
P.P.S. Don't tell Father!!!

Matthew will never guess that I'm living in Mama's kitchen garden.
Though this doesn't look like the garden from before, when Mama was still alive.
It's overgrown here.
It's crowded here. There's no more room!

Where is the grass I played on?
Sometimes Mama spread out a blanket, and we would sit on it and sing together…I can still remember Matthew lying nearby in his baby carriage.
Now a bush grows there!
And Auntie Mame, Mama's old doll!
I'd forgotten about her. I wonder where she is now.
I remember I was allowed to hold her sometimes.
"Just for a moment, with cotton-soft hands," Mama used to say. "Very, very carefully."
I can't keep the garden like this, if I want to live here.
I'm going to make it the way it used to be.

It really is quiet, though…Who can I talk to?

I wish I still had a mother!

But she hasn't gone away.
If I listen carefully,
I can still hear her
in the rustling wind,
in the whispering grass.
She sings in the trees.
That's what all people do
who were loved
when they lived.

Who's there?
It's me, Matthew.
What do you want?
Hannah wants me to get a basket.
She went to live somewhere else
and so she needs some things.
How unexpected—what a surprise!
I didn't think that anyone would
ever be allowed in here.

It's not allowed, but Father says
I always have to do what my sister says.
And she knew where the key was:
in front of the door, under the mat.
That's where I found it.
Then get the basket
and take it to Hannah.
See you again, Matthew.
Bye-bye, Voice of Mama.

My little girl, here you are!
How did you get into my garden?
I thought the gate was closed forever.
I crawled through a hole, Mama,
where a stone was loose.
And from now on,
this is where I plan to live.
Well, well, you ran away!
You did too, Mama dear!

And that was worse,
because you died.
Ah, dead, what is dead? It's only a word
for when you're not seen and when you're not heard.
My voice locked up,
the keys hidden.
My room shut and my garden closed.
What could I do to make you hear me?
I thought I wasn't allowed to speak anymore!

I don't care that Hannah's gone, she's too bossy anyway. I always have to do everything for her.
Maybe I'll practice writing now.
But first I'll read the story…

Once upon a time there were a king and a queen who said to each other every day, "Oh, if only we had a child." But after many years, they were still childless.

Then one spring day, as the queen walked in the garden picking flowers, a little rose spoke to her: "If you spare me, I'll fulfill your dearest wish by tomorrow morning."

Flowers can't talk, so this is a stupid story.

The queen spared the rose and went home. When she returned to the garden the next day, she suddenly heard a child crying. She parted the bushes and saw a beautiful little girl, exactly where the rose grew the day before. The queen picked up the child, who immediately threw her arms around the queen's neck. Overjoyed, the queen returned home with her.

"Look, our dearest wish has been fulfilled," she said to the king. But the king was shocked to see scratches on the queen's neck. He wanted nothing to do with a child that hurt her mother like that.

The queen took the little girl to her room. "Show me your nails," she said, and brought out a pair of scissors to cut the needle-sharp thorns. But the girl started to cry heartbreakingly; she hid her hands and looked at her mother with reproach. So the queen threw the scissors out of the window and never tried to cut the girl's nails again.

Day and night, the queen stayed with the child, whom she called Rosa, after the flower she resembled in so many ways. But when the princess was ten years old, the queen died. The king ordered Rosa, unloved by anyone except her mother, to be locked up in the garden, which was surrounded by a high wall.

And so it happened…

So far I haven't copied anything down.
I don't like that king. It's very sad.
What's this? Another note from Hannah?
I'll read it later.

I need to make sure Matthew gets his meals every day.
He's still too young to cook for himself.
Father needs to eat, too, otherwise he might start
looking for me.
Would he miss me?
I don't think so. He only thinks about his papers.
But how will I cook? There are no pots and pans here,
no knives, no spoons.
I'll have to ask Matthew for them.
I hope he got my note about the table and chairs.
The goat will be a big help with such heavy things.
And vegetables? Where will I get vegetables?
If I get rid of the nettles, the weeds, and all the dead
branches, maybe I'll find something.

Mama was always working here.
She planted, she picked, she trimmed, she cut.
Let's see, what used to be over there?
I only remember the tree with the yellow blossoms,
because Mama often sat under it.
And of course the apple tree, because my swing hung
there.
When the swing broke, Father promised to hang it up
again. But he never did.
I was almost seven then, I think. Like Matthew now.
I really hope he does his homework every day.
Otherwise he'll be sorry later.
"Auntie Mame! How lucky to have you here! Now I
have someone to play with."

"Father, a princess was standing on the wall last night."

"Princesses do not exist, Matthew."

"They do too, look in my book.

"She was just like this one."

"I think you dreamed it, son. How is your homework coming along?"

Hey, what's that clip-clopping sound?
It's the goat carrying something back from Hannah!

Dear Matthew,
In the you-know-what is a green dresser with a mirror and a little stool. I need them tonight. Be careful with the glass!

Hannah

"Stay away, Koos, that's Father's bowl."

He didn't see her, but I did. I don't think I dreamed it.

"Father! Dinner!"

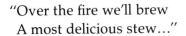

"Over the fire we'll brew
A most delicious stew…"

"Well, you sure came back fast! Stay away! You didn't eat my note, I hope. Because I need a mirror awfully badly."

Maybe I shouldn't burn too many branches all at once.
The smoke will blow over the wall.
Suppose Matthew happened to look this way—
he might figure out that I'm here!

Tomorrow I'll make rice with chicken. Yummy.
When it's ready, Koos can take it over to the house.
Though Koos loves chicken!
I'll have to think of something so he can't eat it on the way.
Hmm…That little fire is just what I need to keep me warm for now…

Matthew, here you are again!
What did you come to get this time?
I think Hannah wants the green dresser with the
minnow, or is it mirror? And the little stool
but be careful with the glass.
I couldn't quite read the note because
her writing was so messy.
What did you do with the chairs and the table?
Last night, while Father slept, I took them to the ditch.

Afterward, when I peeked around the back door,
do you know what I saw on top of the garden wall?
A princess.
How did you guess?
I did not guess. I just happened to say it.
Get the dresser with the mirror, quick,
and take it to Hannah.
See you later, little Matthew.
Bye-bye, Voice of Mama.

Good morning, Hannah.
Is that you, Mama?
I hope you don't mind if I ask you
about picking all those apples.
What are you going to do?
I'm going to make apple stew and apple salad.
And applesauce for dessert.
The rest I'll roast in the fire.
Don't forget to eat vegetables, too!
I can decide that for myself.

I don't want to meddle, my child,
but are you getting enough sleep?
How can I sleep well?
The grass is wet at night.
The nettles sting me.
The ground is hard as stone
and crawling with ants.
Can we do something about it?
I'll think of something. Yes, I know.
I'll send another note.

"WHO IS MAKING ALL THAT NOISE?"

If the princess stands on the wall again tonight,
I'll call to her, "Rosa, is that you?"
If she says yes, then I'll know it's her.

As she grew accustomed to her stone prison, Rosa learned how to satisfy her hunger. By shaking a tree, she could make ripe apples fall to the ground.

Yes, that must be the tree in Mama's kitchen garden. Sometimes Hannah picks up the apples that drop in the grass outside the wall. But they have worms.

From the bushes she picked berries and grapes, and she dug up turnips and carrots from the ground with her nails.

Hannah can't dig up turnips because she always bites her nails. Where was I? Oh yes…

When autumn came, the wild storms caused nuts to rain down from the trees. The princess stacked them in a corner of the garden, so she would not go hungry in the coming winter.

With fallen branches, she built a hut to protect herself against the cold. She filled the holes and cracks with moss and clumps of grass.

I made a hut too, once, when cousin Billy stayed with us. I was only five then. We built it together.
Billy took boxes from Father's room. "Billy," I said, "you can't do that," but he did it anyway. Then the papers in the boxes got wet, because all of a sudden it started to rain awfully hard. Father was really mad at him and gave him a spanking. That's why he never wants to stay with us—Billy—and now I'm always by myself during vacation.

One day, a yearling jumped over the wall. At first the princess was surprised. She gently reached out to touch him, and the yearling responded by snuggling up against her.

What is a yearling?
I'll have to go ask Father, otherwise I won't know what the story is about.
Hmm…I wonder if it's getting dark outside yet.

Someday I'm going to live near the sea.
There aren't as many weeds there.
I'll have a little house and lots of roses.
Yellow ones only; I think they're the prettiest.
I'll also have a grownup to run the house.
Someone like Aunt Willa. She can work
awfully hard.
Maybe I'll let Matthew come, too. We'll send him and
cousin Billy off to catch fish.
I heard if you eat a lot of fish you don't need as
many vegetables.
Aunt Willa is such a good cook: codfish with fried
onions, carrot stew with bacon strips, turnips with
melted butter…and oatmeal with raisins!
Yum…

Once we looked for blackberries together.
She baked them in a pie for teatime.
Back then our home still smelled like Mama's home.
If Father hadn't given cousin Billy a spanking, Aunt
Willa would have stayed with us.

Would blackberries grow near the sea?

Once Aunt Willa sent me a book.
My favorite book. It has a story about a princess with
very sharp nails.
I hope Matthew takes good care of it.
I should write him not to make folds in the pages,
not to touch them with sticky fingers.
Otherwise he'll be in big trouble.

It smells like food in here.
"Hannah, is that you?
"HANNAH!"

"Come back, Koos! You can't
go across the ditch. It's
much too dangerous."
Oh well, let him.

"Father, did you hear
anything last night?"
"I hear nothing at night
because I'm asleep."
"Didn't you see Hannah?"
"No, I didn't."
"Then what about the
food?"

"I have no idea, son."
"And who tied the scarf
around Koos's nose?"
"He must have done it
himself. Why don't you go
and play? Can't you see I'm
busy?"

There's something I don't
get. I don't understand
what's going on with
Hannah. She's living
somewhere, but where?
Maybe she built a hut
somewhere in the forest.
Lots of branches broke off
during the last storm. But
what about the chicken and
rice? And the scarf around
Koos's nose?

"Jeepers, Koos! Look what you're doing! Get out of here with your dirty paws! I'll never get done."

Well, I'll pick those berries later.
My dress needs to be washed, anyway.
And yours too, Auntie Mame!
Oh yuck, mine has so many grass stains!
How can I get rid of them?
White gets dirty so fast!
I think I'll dye the dress black one day.

Auntie Mame is angry!
"Come on now, listen to me! What good is it to have a nice clean dress when you smell like a skunk? There now!"

My dear little Matthew, why in such a hurry?
We didn't have a chance to talk to each other!
How are things with your father?
No time, no time, because Hannah writes
that I have to get the sofa right away.
Otherwise she can't sleep.
She lies on the ground in the forest at night.
Wild animals roam around there.
And that is very dangerous.

Can you remember how it was before,
when you were lying in your mother's arms?
She taught you songs. She fed you.
How should I know that?
I forgot it.
Before is so long ago!
Go and do quickly what your sister asked.
See you again, Matthew.
Bye-bye, Voice of Mama.

How is my little princess today?
You'd better not bother me,
because I'm very busy
with laundry and the rest.
I picked berries
and made berry tea.
Maybe you want a cup?
I'm going to have one.
I'm feeling a little cold.

Do you still think of Father sometimes?
Don't mention him.
How for heaven's sake can I dry that dress!
I wish the wind would start to blow.
The wind is a fickle gentleman.
Sometimes he hides, and then
he creates a racket again.
He does more or less what he wants to do,
but I could ask him to do a favor for you.

"NO ROLLER-SKATING IN THE HALL!"

There's always a voice in that room.
I'm not telling Father because he'll just say rooms can't talk. They can, though; I heard it myself.
Flowers can talk, too.
It says so in my book, and whatever a book says is true.
The princess is real and she's in the book.
I didn't see her yesterday—I yelled really loud, "Rosa, are you there?" but she didn't answer.
I think I'll read some more…

Sleeping on a bed of straw at night and playing inside the high walls during the day, Rosa and the yearling spent the winter together. There was plenty of food in the garden for them both.

I get it. She was lying on her bed of straw last night. That's why she couldn't hear me.
Father says a yearling is a young deer that lives in the forest. "Did you see one?" he said, and I said yes.

But when the snow began to melt and the garden echoed with birdsong, the yearling became restless. He kept jumping up against the wall and cried out plaintively.

Why would he want to get out?

"Dear God, let him stay with me," the princess prayed, but her prayer was not heard. One morning, when she woke up, the yearling was gone. No matter where she looked, no matter where she called, she did not find him.

I know. I'll make a drawing for her with greetings from Matthew. I'll let it blow away in the wind.
What if it blows the wrong way, and floats off toward the forest?
What will Hannah think if she finds it?
Will she answer?

Someday I'm going to live in the mountains.
Yes, that's a good idea.
There are goats everywhere in the mountains.
I read that once.
Then I can choose a different one,
because ours is such a nuisance.
When I need her, she's running around outside.
When I don't need her, she gets in my way.
Or she's eating lettuce behind my back.
I always have to keep an eye on her!
When you want to milk a goat in the mountains, you
simply step outside and…gotcha!
The mountains would be good for Matthew, too.
He could learn to be a goatherd.

Then I wouldn't have to worry about him anymore.
But of course he'll need a flute.
I can easily cut one out of wood.
There's plenty of wood in the mountains
because there are lots of forests.
Would there be wolves and bears, too?
Or maybe birds of prey? Big ones with those strong
claws!
Sometimes they carry little children off to their nests.
I read that once.
That would mean you could never go outside.
Far too dangerous!

Maybe…

"Father, you never believe me, do you?"

"Yes I do, when you don't talk utter nonsense."

"Do princesses sometimes live in regular houses? And are they strong enough to pull a sofa up over a wall?"

"Oh yes."

"Father?"

"What is it this time?"

"It's not really dangerous to cross the ditch, is it?"

"No, it is not."

"Well, I'm off."

Everything needs to be clean when Rosa comes.
Tonight I'm going to find her.
Then we can play together.
I'm sure she doesn't have sharp nails anymore.

"Rosa really pulled the sofa up, Koos.
Hannah will be mad, because she wanted it."

"Who baked the bread?
It is the mother who did it.
That's not true, it's not true,
because the mother is dead.

"Who washed the clothes?
It was the mother who did it.
That was true, it was true,
when she was still with us.

"Who read your books to you?
I read them to myself.
That is true, it is true
I'm a grown-up girl now.

"And why doesn't your father?
I asked him to do it,
but he doesn't listen!"

"I have to do everything all by myself!
Auntie Mame, you just sit there on the sofa—
and it's already so heavy!
Do you know what would be fun, Auntie Mame?
If you were big. As big as I am, for example.
Then you could help me push…
Next May I'll put you out in the rain.
It'll make you grow, did you know that?
I know a song about it.
Anyway, we don't have to sleep on the
ground anymore.
At least that's something!"

It really makes no difference to me,
but I'd like to know
why my piano has to go.

My little Matthew, can't you hear me?
I hear you, but I'm not listening
because I'm so very busy.
It's not right that a boy of six
has to drag along this heavy load!

Please leave me alone, it's not heavy
and I'm almost seven, anyway.
What has gotten into Hannah's head?
She doesn't even know how to play it!
Wrong, wrong, if you think the piano is for Hannah.
I need it for the princess.
And you don't need to know any more.
Bye-bye, Voice of Mama.
All right, Matthew. See you again.

How well you have arranged it,
my garden and my room all in one.
The sky as roof and the grass as carpet.
If only Father and Matthew could see it!

Hannah!…Hannah, are you sleeping?
I'm not asleep and I won't listen.
I don't want to hear a word. Because I moved in here
and Father and Matthew have to stay out!

That's what she thinks,
she will not be told
anything, my little eleven-year-old.
No worries today; it is summer now,
with fruit in the trees, berries below.
But what will happen tomorrow,
when the summer wind disturbs her dream?
Child, who can stop that happening?
Who speaks the language of the wind?

"NOT SO NOISY DOWN THERE!"

It's okay that the yearling is gone.
Now that Rosa's alone, she'll be glad to see me.
I'll say, "I've come to get you!"
But now I'm very hot from pushing this piano.
Tonight, when I've pushed it to the wall,
I'll climb on top of it and yell,
"Princess Rosa! Would you like to live with us?"
Then she'll call back, "How do you know my name?"
And I'll say, "You're in my book."
Then I'll give her the book
so she can read the story for herself.

Princess Rosa, inconsolable, walked back and forth along the walls of the garden. She barely ate. Her cheeks grew pale and gradually she lost her strength.

With that sofa yesterday she seemed quite strong.

Not until summer did she revive, finally accepting her fate. She shaped pots from clay and let them dry in the sun. She kindled a fire with dry twigs and branches and cooked the most delicious meals. What she did not eat herself she left for the field mice, ferrets, birds, and insects. She picked flowers and gathered them in bouquets.

I'm going to pick flowers, too.
I'll put them in Rosa's room—the one that used to be Hannah's.

One evening toward the end of the summer, the princess heard the sound of thudding hooves on the soft ground behind her. She whirled around and there she saw, between the apple tree and the wall, the yearling, now grown into a beautiful stag.

She ran over, and the stag knelt down. Rosa hugged him as tears of joy flowed from her eyes and rolled down his soft coat. Then the animal slowly stood up and said, "I have come to take you away from here."

Yes, that's me! Just wait, Rosa. I'm coming!

When I grow up I'll become a singer, I think.
Then I'll sing all the songs I learned from Mama.
If you want to become a singer, you have to practice
a lot.
So you need a piano.
I can't ask Matthew for that.
It's much too heavy for a little boy his age.
And where would I put it? Outside against the wall?
I could build a shed around it. That's not so difficult.
Just hammer some boards together.
What if I saved my white dress and sewed
glittery beads on it?
Then I can wear it when I sing.
And what kind of shoes would go with it?
Wait a minute, in Mama's closet…
those white ones with the heels!

I wish I had those shoes here already. I could keep
them in the wicker basket. Then nothing could happen
to them.

Sometimes Matthew plays with matches.
There's nobody to really keep an eye on him now.
Suppose there's a fire. Then my shoes will be lost.
I should make sure to ask for them.
Where's my pen?

Maybe I'll become a writer, too…
I could start that right away.
I can make up enough stories. That's easy.
Besides, if you write your own stories you'll never
need to buy a book or get one as a present.
Yes, that's what I'll do.

I forgot to bring the story.

She might not find the story in the book, so I ripped it out of my notebook.

"She's coming back with me, she's not coming back with me…

coming back with me, not coming back with me…

coming… AAAAAH!"

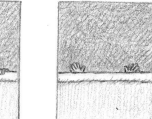

I'll put the papers under the piano cover. Now they can't blow away.

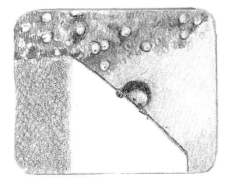

"I'll teach you, goat! I'll teach you!"
"Stop! Matthew, stop! You torturer of animals!"

"The goat ate the story… there's only a little bit left…"
"What story?"
"The story of the princess!"
"What princess?"
"Rosa…you!…No… Hannah!"

"Huh? Come quickly behind the wall. The wind is really picking up."

Hey, where did the papers go?

"Did you eat them?"

From the top of the ladder in the garden, Hannah and Matthew could see Father. He was carried by the wind across the yard, with all his papers flying every which way.

"Watch out!" Hannah yelled. "You're going to hit the wall!" But the bricks that had covered the entrance to the kitchen garden were all loose, and suddenly Father was in the garden, too!

The two children hurried down the ladder.

"Father, are you hurt?" asked Hannah.

"Oh no," he said, though he seemed dazed. He thought he was back in the house. "Oh dear, the roof blew off!" he said. "Tomorrow I'll repair it."

Then Father turned to Matthew. "Did you remember to copy the story, my boy?" he asked, and Matthew explained how the goat had eaten it.

"Well, don't worry," said Father, "I lost all my papers, too."

"Shall I go pick them up for you?" asked Matthew.

"No, I've had enough of those papers," he said. "I'm glad they're finally gone."

They all sat around the fire for a very long time until Matthew yawned. "I'm going to sleep now, because this day has tired me out." And Hannah and Father went to sleep, too.

The next morning, Father was the first one up.

"What a terrible wind last night! Every now and then it starts to blow like that. Wake up, children! Do you remember when, a while back, the roof of the chicken coop blew off? But then it rained, too. Not like last night. There was no rain at all—just wind—what a windstorm! I must repair the roof…"

Mama asked the wind for a favor, thought Hannah. Now the whole family is here, together. I might as well forget about the sea and everything else.
In no time, things will be just as they always were:
Can you do this, Hannah?
Would you mind doing that?
What about this? What about that?
Well, I'm not going along with it anymore!
They can't make me do anything.
Not Matthew! Not Father!
And I can do without that voice, too.

Nobody is left
in the empty house.
A cabinet full of stories
and furniture made of shadows.
There isn't much there anymore.
The tea in the pot
on the lowest shelf
got cold and the clock
on the upper shelf stopped
at a quarter to ten.

But Koos chases the cat, who chases a pigeon.
And the goat with her amber gaze
and her pale beard watches them
through the half-open door.
She would not mind tasting a leaf
of a rustling, crackling children's book.
But she prefers to wait till night,
when the other animals have disappeared.
Then she can take time to savor each bite,
without getting in trouble afterward.

Matthew is sleeping.
Father is building a roof of old boards
over the kitchen garden.
Hannah sets the table with candles and flowers.
"Would you like to start with soup, Father?" she asks.
And her cheeks are streaked with tears.
Hiding place gone, she has to take care of everything again.
Doing the same things
she always did.
You can bet Father won't answer her!

But then he says, with his mouth full of nails,
"Yes, please, my girl. What would I do without you!"

No, things aren't at all as they used to be.
And Hannah smiles, just a little.

Besides, whoever wants to run away
will find, on the other side of the yard,
a yellow stone house, with its door
swinging in the breeze.